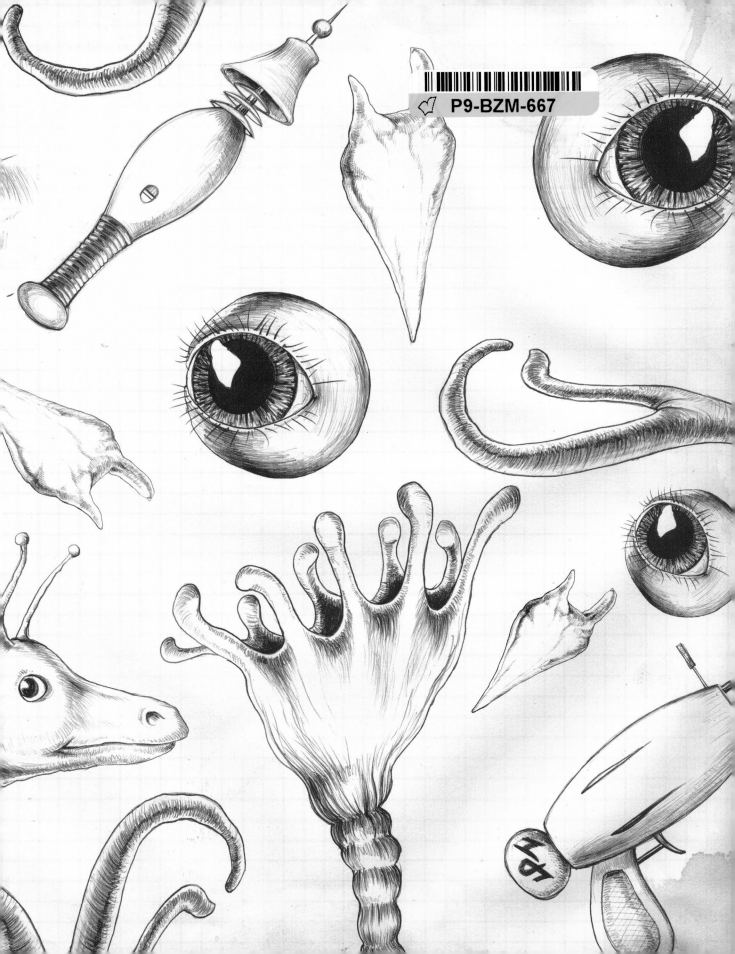

FOR VIVIENNE AND OLIVIA

Text and illustrations copyright © 2010 by Johan Olander

Marshall Cavendish Corporation, 99 White Plains Road, Tarrytown, NY 10591
www.marshallcavendish.us/kids

Library of Congress Cataloging-in-Publication Data
Olander, Johan.
A field guide to aliens : intergalactic worrywarts, bubblonauts, sliver-slurpers, and
other extraterrestrials / observations and illustrations by world-famous monstrologist Johan Olander. 1st ed.
p. cm.
Summary: Reports the habitat, diet, lifecycle, and other characteristics of a variety
of unusual creatures from other planets, as observed and recorded by a monstrologist.
ISBN 978-0-7614-5594-3
1. Extraterrestrial beings—Fiction. 2. Imaginary creaturesFiction.—I. Title.
PZ7.O4233Fic 2007
Ficdc22
2009005936

The images on pages 39 and 55 are from NASA/courtesy of nasaimages.org.
The illustrations are rendered in ink, pencil, watercolor, and oil paint on
various papers and boards. Color additions and enhancements
created with Adobe Photoshop.

Book design by Kristen Branch / Michael Nelson Design
Editor: Marilyn Mark

Printed in Malaysia (T)
First edition
1 3 5 6 4 2

mc Marshall Cavendish
Children

A FIELD GUIDE TO ALIENS

INTERGALACTIC WORRYWARTS, BUBBLONAUTS,
SLIVER-SLURPERS, AND OTHER EXTRATERRESTRIALS

OBSERVATIONS AND ILLUSTRATIONS BY
WORLD-FAMOUS MONSTROLOGIST

JOHAN OLANDER

Marshall Cavendish
Children

LETTER TO MY READERS

DEAR FELLOW HUMAN AND/OR LITERATE ALIEN,

I am proud to present you with the first truly comprehensive field guide of alien visitors to Earth.

Most of you know me as the world's foremost authority on monsters, and as such I am often called upon to investigate mysterious creatures all over the world. However, monsters are not the only beings that lurk in the shadows. My research has made it clear that about forty-five percent of the monsters reported are actually aliens. This has been a challenge for me and has led to some confusion. The need for a field guide of similar depth and professionalism as my seminal work, *A FIELD GUIDE TO MONSTERS*, became apparent. So after years of dangerous missions, relentless scorn from mainstream science, warm support from the alien-affected public, and a few die-hard colleagues, here it is!

— *A FIELD GUIDE TO ALIENS* —

A BRIEF INTRODUCTION TO THE SCIENCE OF ALIENOLOGY

This guide presents aliens that are found in that fertile land where few grown-up scientists dare to tread; it is that same area where monsters can be found. A zone of endless possibilities and bottomless fear, it is the borderland between fantasy and reality. This area is fed by impulses from culture, nature, and your imagination. In order to document these beings, one must enter this special zone of perception.

I am proud to have what it takes to do this highly specialized task:

• an open mind

• a vivid imagination

• a keen eye for observation

As long as you maintain these three things, and combine them in the right doses, you can do it, too!

THE ALIEN HUNT

There are a few tools of the trade that can be helpful when you're hunting for aliens. Some aliens are exceedingly shy, while others are extremely aggressive, so it is always a good idea to plan your mission well. You will need:

• notebook and pencils (Make sure to bring several well-sharpened pencils. It can be terrifying in the field, and pencil-tips break easily when your hands tremble.)

• flashlight (Bring extra batteries, although do not bring too many! Some aliens, like the Zappy, eat electricity and are dangerous to humans.)

• old blanket or sheet

• battery-operated radio (preferably with headphones)

As with the hunt for monsters, when you're investigating aliens it is helpful to bring a writing/drawing tool as well as something to hide under, like an old blanket or sheet. You might need to cut eye-holes in your cover (make sure it's okay with whoever is in charge of the linens and blankets in your household).

A flashlight is essential for making field notes and sketches while under cover.

A radio is a unique tool for use in the search for extra-terrestrials. By listening to the changes in the static between radio stations, you can detect whether there is some kind of alien activity in the area. Of course, it's an art to discern what kind of changes might indicate an alien, but once trained, this skill can give you that important "heads-up" before an alien enters the scene.

So sharpen your pencils, open your minds, tune your radios to static, and let's go alien hunting!

— Johan Olander
SENIOR MONSTROLOGIST AND ALIENOLOGIST

The Mulchon

NAME IN NATIVE LANGUAGE *Phrruii Phruii rzzz*

ORIGIN
The exact origin of the Mulchon is not known, but most alienologists assume that these aliens come from a planet that has been cleared of all trees.

DIET
This alien's diet seems to consist exclusively of trees.

DISTINGUISHING FEATURES
Mulchons look almost lizard-like and their size varies: a starving Mulchon might be 5 feet tall, but a well-fed one can easily be triple that in size. They have three fingers and toes with retractable claws.

Despite the Mulchon's friendly appearance, this alien avoids humans. Mulchons are not dangerous, but if you find yourself between a Mulchon and a tree, you'd better step out of the way. The real problem with the Mulchon is that it eats trees, leaving behind vast destruction.

Mulchons' jaws open extremely wide, and their bodies can absorb an enormous mass of wood. They can eat and digest whole trees in a matter of minutes. Unfortunately, it has also been discovered that they take loads of lumber with them when they leave Earth.

Their name, given to them by lumberjacks, refers to their droppings, which both look and act as an excellent pest- and weed-resistant mulch.

MULCHONIAN LASER SAW WITH ADJUSTABLE FLAME LENGTH

ALIEN SIGHTINGS ON EARTH

The Mulchon are often seen by lonely lumberjacks deep in the woods. These aliens generally avoid cities and humans, most likely in order to focus entirely on trees.

The drawing, Fig. A below, was made by Hank Swenson, a fifty-six-year-old lumberjack working alone in the forests of Alaska. He claims that the two Mulchons he observed cleared a square mile of pine forest in less than an hour, leaving behind nothing but short stumps. He described their voracious appetite in the following way: "They ate like they had wood chippers in their jaws and put a whole tree away in less time than it takes me to eat an apple."

Some who have encountered this alien claim that it can communicate with humans through charades.

TECHNOLOGY

Although their spaceships look rather crude, the Mulchon's technology is quite advanced. These trucks travel at velocities up to three times the speed of light. It is not known what fuel powers these vehicles, but they emit a strong diesel-like odor.

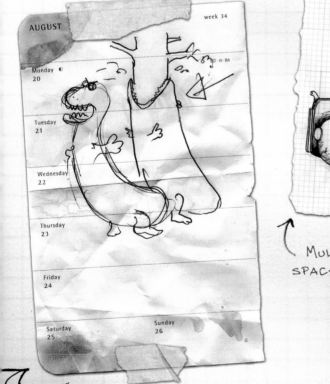

MULCHONIAN SPACE TRUCK

FIG. A
MULCHONS EMPLOY AN EFFICIENT LASER SAW THAT CUTS LARGE TREES AS IF THEY WERE STRAWS OF GRASS. THE MULCHON CAN THEN USE ITS POWERFUL CLAWS TO GRAB THE TREE AND INGEST IT AS SHOWN IN FIG. B, OR LOAD IT ONTO THEIR SPACE TRUCKS FOR TRANSPORT BACK TO THEIR HOME PLANET.

FIG. B
A MULCHON'S JAW OPENS VERY WIDE TO ENGULF TREES FROM THE BOTTOM UP.

Cloudian

DANGER TO HUMANS

NAME IN NATIVE LANGUAGE	The sound of thunder
ORIGIN	This alien originates somewhere in deep, empty space, but it has no home planet.
DIET	Cloudians absorb water vapor.
DISTINGUISHING FEATURES	The intense curiosity of the Cloudians makes these aliens extremely dangerous. Their long, lashing tongues can pluck things off the ground or out of the skies. If, for example, an airplane catches its fancy, a Cloudian might grab and hold it for anywhere from seconds to years. (Cloudians operate on a different idea of time; a minute or a year seems to make no difference to them.) For people who have survived after being held by the Cloudians, time appears to have stood still. Andrew McLeod of Aberdeen, Scotland, lost 29 pounds after what he described as "fainting for a spell" while driving to visit his newborn niece in 2006. When he was found six weeks later, Andrew was very, very hungry but otherwise well. He has no memory of the Cloudians but feels quite good about the weight loss.

ALIEN SIGHTINGS ON EARTH	The Cloudians are one of the most common extraterrestrial visitors to Earth. They are abundant in the skies all over the planet, but their perfect camouflage makes them almost impossible to spot. One way to discern them from regular clouds is by their eyes and tongues. However, these can be difficult to see since they only appear for milliseconds and can pop out anywhere on the Cloudian's body. A more reliable method is to use radar. Cloudians do not show up on radar, so if the weather radar shows clear blue skies and you see big, billowing clouds, there's a good chance that you are observing Cloudians.
TECHNOLOGY	Cloudians do not use any technology. They are completely self-sufficient and travel through space in their cloud form, linked together in groups of four to ten clouds. The drawing below was made in 1974 by an unnamed Russian cosmonaut who says he saw this cluster of "clouds" drifting away from Earth toward Mars.

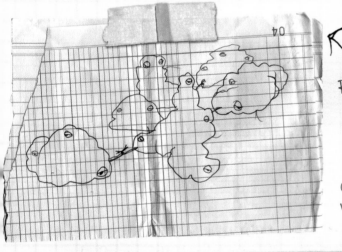

A HASTY DRAWING MADE BY THE UNNAMED RUSSIAN COSMONAUT

I FOUND THIS COLLAGE OF A CLOUDIAN, MADE BY 6-YEAR-OLD MAX SCHNABEL, IN A 1ST-GRADE ART SHOW IN MIAMI, FLORIDA. ⟶

THIS SEASCAPE PAINTING WAS BROUGHT BACK AS A SOUVENIR BY MY SISTER AFTER SHE VISITED GAMBIA IN WEST AFRICA. SHE THOUGHT IT WAS JUST A PRETTY PICTURE. I BELIEVE IT DEPICTS FIVE CLOUDIANS, DUE TO THE WAY THE "CLOUDS" APPEAR LINKED TOGETHER.

Strunt

NAME IN NATIVE LANGUAGE *Strunt-von-Excela-Exclama-Grandolinior-el-Maj-e-Haq-von-Lööf-af-Leuwee-Pransing-Cultivatoriam*

ORIGIN

Strunt do not have a home planet. They live on large spaceliners in a militaristic society.

The most plausible theory on their origin is that of my colleague Dr. Hasbien, who believes the Strunt actually come from Earth. According to Hasbien, in the fall of 1868 there were top-secret experiments taking place in Prussia. Leading military scientists were trying to create a space-faring ship to fight back against alien attacks rumored to be imminent. Of course, the alien attacks never happened. But Dr. Hasbien believes that the group of scientists succeeded in creating a space vehicle, climbed inside, launched it, and promptly got lost in space. The crew became the founders of the Strunt civilization. Because of their focus on the technological sciences, there were no historians or writers in the group. Dr. Hasbien believes they lost any memory of their origin within one generation and now only visit Earth by chance.

DIET

Strunt eat a tofu-like substance called "nutra," which they produce on their ships using human waste material.

DISTINGUISHING FEATURES

The Strunt look human and wear elaborate uniforms. These aliens have been lost in space for many generations. (In alienology circles, the Strunt are known as "the flying Dutchmen" of deep space.) This is primarily due to the Strunts' prideful ways; they just will not ask anybody for help along the way.

Their visits on planets seem observational. They rarely interact with natives, whom the Strunt always treat as inferior to themselves, no matter how advanced the observed species might be.

ALIEN SIGHTINGS ON EARTH

Strunt sightings have been made all over Earth. There were a slew of sightings in South America from 1960 to the late 1980s. In 1976 meteorologist Santiago Farsical of the Argentine Navy observed a Strunt spaceliner and interacted with a Struntian officer. They used a mix of languages to communicate. The Strunt called Farsical "a lowly flea-hound unable to talk proper Struntian, but in spite of this perhaps Monsieur Flea-Hound was abilitized to facilitate a chalice de aqua." (Basically, the Strunt used a long-winded, offensive way to ask for a glass of water.) Señor Farsical explains what happened next:

"Since he did not grant me any form of civil greeting, I naturally declined to give him water. The Strunt then called me even worse things and asked again for water. I declined and told him that he was not providing me with the proper respect, given my position as a meteorologist and major of the Argentine Navy." (Señor Farsical's telling is itself very long-winded.)

The two men continued arguing until both claimed to have won the dispute, and they parted ways. Farsical made good field drawings of the Strunt and its technology after the encounter.

TECHNOLOGY

Strunt technology looks primitive but is advanced. These aliens have many different devices for navigation (since finding their way has been a big problem for them).

Their spaceliners are self-contained systems capable of interstellar flight for many generations without repair, restocking, or refueling. Nobody knows how they do it.

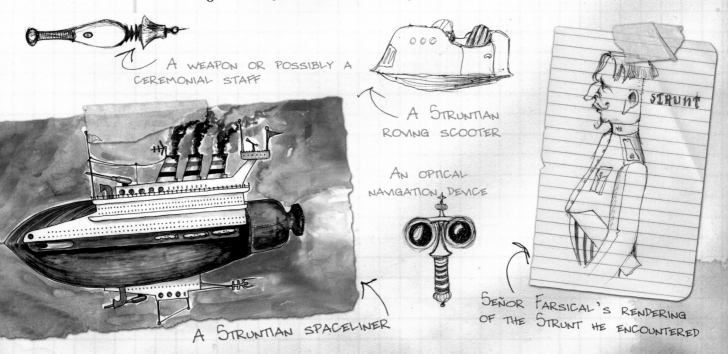

A WEAPON OR POSSIBLY A CEREMONIAL STAFF

A STRUNTIAN ROVING SCOOTER

AN OPTICAL NAVIGATION DEVICE

A STRUNTIAN SPACELINER

SEÑOR FARSICAL'S RENDERING OF THE STRUNT HE ENCOUNTERED

False Santa

RADICAL NEW THEORY ON SANTA CLAUS INTRODUCED BELOW

NAME IN NATIVE LANGUAGE *Tomtenisse*

ORIGIN	False Santas come from a planet in the galaxy surrounding Stella Polaris, The North Star.
DIET	The False Santa's diet consists primarily of gingerbread, fruitcake, nuts, clementines, cookies, and milk.
DISTINGUISHING FEATURES	The False Santa's appearance is very similar to that of Santa Claus. However, False Santas are sterner looking and much less animated when seen up close. In fact, much of what makes False Santas look like Santa Claus is the protective gear they use for their space travel (see Technology). In addition, their feet have only one pointy and upward-curling toe. Most alienologists assume that the character under the "disguise" is in fact a group of beings that more closely resembles Santa's helpers, the elves. The Christmas fanatic Jim G. Bells claims that the False Santas are a rogue group of Santaland elves, but he has no evidence whatsoever for this theory.

14

ALIEN SIGHTINGS ON EARTH

False Santas visit Earth at Christmastime. The discovery of this alien has led researchers to rethink the theory of Santa Claus's origin. Dr. J. S. Poiler, the first to have seen False Santas, believes they have been coming to Earth for many years, posing as the real Santa Claus. He does not know whether the actual Santa Claus exists but claims that most Santa Claus sightings are False Santas. The impostors do not bring gifts; instead, they harvest the treats found in abundance on earth at this time of year.

Jennifer Hamparian, eight years old, of Westchester, New York, blames these aliens for the missing chocolate chip cookies in her home last year. She believes they entered and exited the house through her bedroom window, which would explain the trail of cookie crumbs leading to her room.

TECHNOLOGY

False Santas have a variety of fascinating technology. Their red cone-shaped hats are helmets. Their beards and mustaches are actually masks with built-in communication technology. Their sleighs are space-yachts of formidable speed.

A SPACE-YACHT, ILLUSTRATION BASED ON DR. J. S. POILER'S EYEWITNESS ACCOUNT. THE TOWED LUGGAGE IS HARVESTED CHRISTMAS SWEETS FROM EARTH.

THIS DRAWING WAS MADE BY DR. J. S. POILER ON AN OLD ENVELOPE ONE CHRISTMAS MORNING AFTER HE WITNESSED A FALSE SANTA TAKE OFF ITS PROTECTIVE GEAR AND STUFF HIMSELF WITH FRUITCAKE.

A HELMET AND MASK THAT WAS LEFT IN DR. J. S. POILER'S LIVING ROOM AFTER HE SCARED THE FALSE SANTA AWAY. THE INTRUDER LEFT WITH HALF A FRUITCAKE, 2 JARS OF COOKIES, 17 CANDY CANES, A LARGE CANDLE THAT LOOKED LIKE A CANDY CANE, AND 2 CLEMENTINES. THE CANDY CANE CANDLE WAS LATER FOUND OUTSIDE THE HOUSE WITH A BITE MARK IN IT.

Rooty

DANGER TO HUMANS

NAME IN NATIVE LANGUAGE A creaking sound, like wood bending

ORIGIN | Rooties originate on the planet Forrs, in the solar system Sylvania.

DIET | The Rooty consumes small animals, especially birds, but has been known to snatch humans who come too close or mistake this dangerous alien for a tree. It is a ruthless predator.

DISTINGUISHING FEATURES | The Rooty has tree-like properties, but where a tree takes months or years to grow a branch, the Rooty seems able to shoot out branches in an instant. This alien can alter its general shape and size greatly, but its head always maintains its distinct shape. The Rooty can disguise itself as a tree and is thus able to lure unsuspecting animals or humans to perch or climb on its "branches" or get close to its "roots." The branches/roots seize the prey and feed it whole to its mouth, which can open as wide as needed to accommodate the size of its victim.

I was able to do some detailed drawings of a Rooty in Prospect Park, Brooklyn. They are a terrifying sight to see, but they are also very shy. If they are called out of their hiding spot, they immediately disappear. They're as frightened of us as we should be of them.

ALIEN SIGHTINGS ON EARTH	Rooties are often found in parks or other areas where there are trees and prey. Ten-year-old Ali Johnston was visiting his uncle and cousins in Salem, Massachusetts, when he spotted a Rooty. "We were playing wiffle-ball in the backyard, and I was in the out-field. Josie hit the ball into the woods. I ran after it but tripped on a root and got tangled up in branches. . . . Then a giant mouth came for me! My scream made the mouth go away. When everyone came over, the trees looked like regular old trees. My cousins teased me . . . but I ain't ever going into those woods again!"
TECHNOLOGY	It's believed that Rooties live together with larger tree-beings that act as their spaceships and home base (see below). It is possible that they employ some kind of mysterious transporter mechanism, since the Rooties can appear and disappear at will. There is no obvious engine or force to propel them or their tree-ships through space. Rooties have never been observed using any tools or devices.

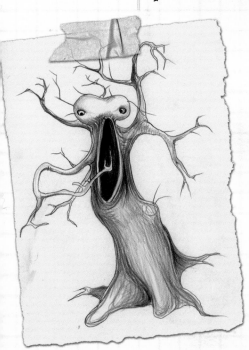

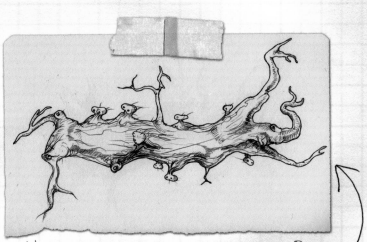

WHEN TRAVELING THROUGH SPACE, THE ROOTIES ARE ATTACHED TO THEIR LARGE TREE-SHIPS, LOOKING LIKE MUSHROOMS.

THE ROOTY I OBSERVED IN PROSPECT PARK, BROOKLYN. NOTE THE CONSISTENT SHAPE OF THE HEAD AND GREAT VARIATION OF THE REST OF THE BODY.

ALI MADE THIS DRAWING AFTER HIS ENCOUNTER WITH THE ROOTY.

Beby

NAME IN NATIVE LANGUAGE *Whaa-haa* (That's the only sound heard from this alien/machine.)

ORIGIN	Unknown
DIET	Like human children, the Beby enjoys sweets, cookies, fruit, milk, and juice. Proper nutrition does not seem to be a priority.
DISTINGUISHING FEATURES	The Beby looks like a robotic human child, allowing it to go unnoticed among kids and their snacks. It is widely accepted that part of the alien is actually a vehicle, an interstellar ship. The vehicle is believed to be controlled by very small aliens of unknown species; because these aliens have rarely been seen outside of the ship, alienologists refer to the machine and its inhabitants collectively as "Beby."

Dr. Somwatnuts, of Bangkok, Thailand, believes that behind the Beby is a cockroach-like alien that he calls the "Chrooch." He claims that he once saw one get out through a Beby's neckline.

Not everybody agrees with Dr. Somwatnuts. UFO specialist Willa Neveno of Roswell, New Mexico, believes the Beby is driven by "the little gray ones," an alien species that she says is the most commonly observed on Earth; she maintains that the Beby is just one of the many vehicles they use to visit Earth.

ALIEN SIGHTINGS ON EARTH	This odd and mysterious alien is often observed near playgrounds and day care centers. The Beby has been spotted in the periphery of these areas, watching young human children at play (undoubtedly looking for opportunities to snatch tasty treats). In many eyewitness accounts, the alien has been seen simply standing still; then all of a sudden it is gone (and so is a baby bottle, juice box, or snack pack). In some rare cases, Bebys have been seen in flight, leading alienologists to the idea of the Beby as a machine/vehicle.
TECHNOLOGY	The Beby itself is the prime example of this alien's technology. It is lifelike in its appearance—but its too-large eyes/windshields and the cold blank stare it gives you are obvious once you get closer. This fast and precise machine can move so quickly that it becomes invisible to human eyes, allowing the Beby to maneuver around a playground and steal stuff. It is also a fully functional spaceship capable of intergalactic travel.

DR. SOMWATNUTS CREATED THIS DRAWING OF THE "CHROOCH."

UFO-SPECIALIST WILLA NEVENO DID THIS DRAWING TO ILLUSTRATE THE SIZE OF "THE LITTLE GRAY ONES," WHO SHE BELIEVES CONTROL THE BEBY.

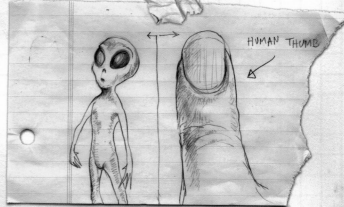

HUMAN THUMB

THIS IS ANOTHER DRAWING BY MS. NEVENO SHOWING THE BEBY IN FLIGHT.

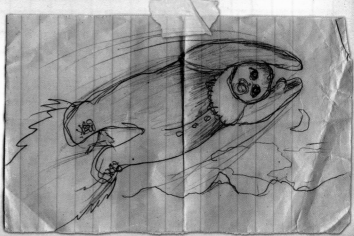

Polkans

NAME IN NATIVE LANGUAGE   These beings refer to themselves in writing as *Polkans* or "we dots." The Polkans do not use sounds, as far as we can tell here on Earth. But while they travel through space it is believed that they make a sound similar to an accordion.

ORIGIN	Polkans are from a planet they call "Polka Prime."
DIET	Polkans consume electromagnetic waves. They seek out strong sources of radiating electricity, such as power stations and radio and TV transmitters. They also seem attracted to large appliance/electronics stores, where lots of electric devices are running at the same time.
DISTINGUISHING FEATURES	The Polkans are light-dots of varying color. They display colors that are part of the normal spectrum, as well as some unnamed colors. It is believed that their colors reflect their moods. Blue and red are very common and are assumed to represent "normal" states. The "dots" are not individuals but part of an immense collective that thinks and feels as one. They have learned several Earth languages and communicate in writing; their words appear floating in space one at a time, which makes it a rather slow process to keep up a conversation. They appear to have a mischievous personality, and their words sometimes cause humorous or embarrassing moments for humans when they read Polkan messages out loud (see example right).

ALIEN SIGHTINGS ON EARTH	Polkans are frequently observed by electronic transmission stations on Earth. They sometimes also sneak into fireworks displays and start writing words. These writings are most often noticed by children. Max Kowalski, a six-year-old from Poland, saw "dots" in the traditional 2004 New Year's Eve fireworks in Gdańsk. He claims that was how he learned a very bad word. "The dots spelled it out in the sky—and I just read it!" An even younger witness, Annie Olsen of Flagstaff, Arizona, made this field drawing in a coloring book when she was three years old. She does not remember the incident, but says she did "a lot of drawings like that."
TECHNOLOGY	Polkans do not use technology. They are pure energy and can exist anywhere. When traveling, they join together as beams of light, creating a powerful laser-like beam that can cut through most known materials like a warm knife through butter. In that form, they can be dangerous to other space travelers.

A FRIENDLY POLKAN MESSAGE
IN THE NIGHT SKY

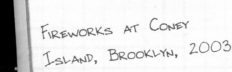

FIREWORKS AT CONEY
ISLAND, BROOKLYN, 2003

"Petkeepers" or Obid with Norri

NAME IN NATIVE LANGUAGE *O-Bid-o-nnri*
(According to the Norri, the Obid is mute)

ORIGIN These aliens live on the planet Norrbi, which is located in a galaxy called Urbia, approximately 200 light years from the Milky Way.

DIET The Obid with Norri eats a varied diet that includes plants, rocks, and metals. They do not eat meat of any kind.

DISTINGUISHING FEATURES You will never see an Obid without at least one Norri, the little creature that the Obids always keep with them.

  The Obids grow to about 5 feet tall and have a streamlined appearance, with few distinguishing characteristics; it can be difficult for humans to tell the difference between individuals. They are nearly completely blind, deaf, and mute.

  The Norri look like a mix between a ferret and a lizard, and they are assumed to act as the eyes and ears of the Obid. They are curious and daring; they dart back and forth between their Obid and the surroundings, continuously feeding information into the Obid's brain through the transponder-like technology that connects them. Thus, the Obid feels, sees, hears, and smells what the Norri feel, see, hear, and smell.

These aliens have been seen in factories and centers of manufacturing. It is believed that the Obid over-evolved and lost track of their ancestral skills and are visiting Earth to reacquaint themselves with basic technology and engineering. Their near blindness and deafness is another consequence of evolution; they became so reliant on their Norri that new Obids were born without their own sight and hearing, proving the accuracy of the famous proverb "use it or lose it."

The term "Petkeepers" came about after encounters with humans in the late fifties and early sixties around Detroit. Fifteen-year-old Jimmy "Dim" DeLussion had a summer job at his uncle's garage and spent hours playing with, and explaining things to, the visiting Obid with Norri.

"The little critters talked in funny squeaky voices, like the chipmunks. They asked me about engines. I told them all I knew about carburetors and gasoline and thingamajigs and such. Dunno if it did them any good. The big fella was always kicking their old spaceship to get it started."

TECHNOLOGY

Obid technology is both highly advanced and very old. It has been endlessly repaired, since none of the Obid remember how to make things from scratch anymore.

A TYPICAL OBID WITH NORRI'S LUNCHBOX. PHOTO BY JIMMY DELUSSION

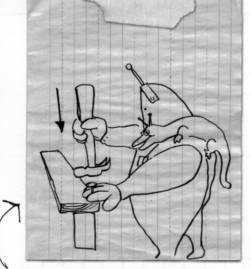

DELUSSION ALSO DESCRIBED TRYING TO TEACH AN OBID TO HAMMER A NAIL. "HE COULDN'T GET IT, HE JUST KEPT HAMMERING THE WRONG WAY AND HITTING HIS THUMB, OR WHATEVER THEY CALL THAT FINGER, OVER AND OVER."

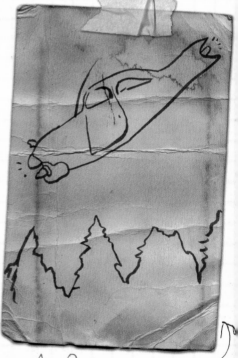

AN OBID SPACE-CAR. DRAWING BY JIMMY DELUSSION

Dolfini

NAME IN NATIVE LANGUAGE *Ne-eh* (pronounced in a squeaky dolphin-like voice)

ORIGIN Dolfini are from a planet in another galaxy— alienologists aren't sure of its exact name. This planet is mostly ocean.

DIET Dolfini eat fish and seaweed.

DISTINGUISHING FEATURES The Dolfini appear to have evolved from dolphins. Their large forehead is the center of their ultrasound ability, similar to the less developed type that Earth's dolphins use. The large eye at the top of their head helps them to distinguish between night and day but not much more.

Their primary sense for experiencing the world is through their use of ultrasound. In light or dark they are able to "see" an image based on how sound is reflected off their environment. It is believed that the Dolfini originated on Earth as a prehistoric dolphin culture, which evolved into a technologically advanced stage during the age of the dinosaurs. They left to find another home planet after they predicted that a massive asteroid was heading toward Earth. Most likely it was this asteroid that caused the extinction of dinosaurs 65 million years ago.

ALIEN SIGHTINGS ON EARTH

Dolfini are usually seen in or near water. However, swimming is not their primary means of transport. They have developed short legs and arms and move like normal bipedal beings, but mostly they cruise around in their state-of-the-art spaceships. Famous observations of these aliens have been made by oil-rig workers and sailors in the Gulf of Mexico. Slim Drillins, a down-on-his-luck oil prospector from Galveston, Texas, claims that he saw a "giant two-legged fish" coming out of a big seafaring vessel during a storm in the Gulf of Mexico. He credits the Dolfini with saving his life since his prospecting boat perished in that storm. Drillins was later spotted on the beach outside the Baha Beach Club, on the eastern tip of Galveston Island.

TECHNOLOGY

The Dolfini's spaceships are equipped with water-filled pods in which the aliens hibernate for extended periods of space travel. These ships are able to travel under water, in air, or in space with no apparent difference in handling.

The Dolfini have also developed efficient sound-weapons that can render an enemy unconscious and deaf.

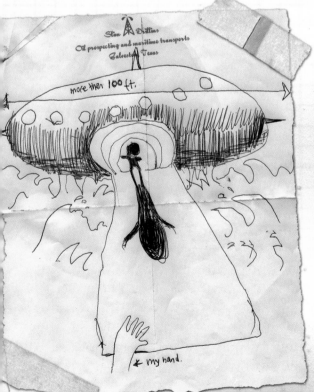

A DOLFINI SOUND-PISTOL. A LIGHT SQUEEZE ON THE BULB EMITS A DEAFENING HONK.

AS REFLECTED IN MANY EXAMPLES OF POPULAR CULTURE, IT IS COMMON KNOWLEDGE THAT A HIGHLY DEVELOPED DOLPHIN CULTURE ONCE EXISTED ON EARTH. THESE WERE LIKELY THE EARLY ANCESTORS OF THE DOLFINI.

SLIM DRILLINS'S DRAMATIC RENDERING OF THE DOLFINI HE WITNESSED.

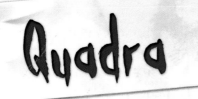

Quadra

NAME IN NATIVE LANGUAGE	*Co'turiste*
ORIGIN	Quadra come from the planet F'shoon in the Drama Galaxy.
DIET	Not known. Quadra have never been seen eating. However, they do enjoy European mineral water.
DISTINGUISHING FEATURES	The Quadra are a slender species with four arms and four legs. They grow to be approximately 6 feet tall but are sometimes considerably taller due to their frequent use of high heels. Quadra dress in what they think is the latest interstellar fashion. They speak many different languages and are not at all shy. Quadra are quite opinionated when it comes to fashion and often make people feel bad about themselves, but otherwise they are not dangerous to humans. There seems to be little difference between male and female Quadra, and either gender can wear whatever feels right as long as the clothing has been deemed "fabulous."

THESE FASHION ILLUSTRATIONS ARE BELIEVED TO HAVE BEEN MADE BY QUADRA, BUT ACCORDING TO EARTH'S FASHIONISTAS, THE STYLE IS STOLEN FROM THE JAPANESE FASHION-DESIGN COMPANY COMMES DES GARÇONS' DESIGNS OF THE LATE 80S.

Quadra have been observed in New York City and Paris during the big annual fashion shows. Fashion seems to be the passion of these aliens and is the driving force behind their interstellar travel.

We know little about these aliens mostly because of their narrow interest in the fashion world. Few in that business even notice that there is an alien among them. José Lafollie, a world-renowned hair stylist, once spent more than twenty minutes with a Quadra. "That leggy thing was wearing a dreadful pantsuit and I must have vented my opinion a bit too loud, 'cause it told me that my *wig* looked phony! My wig! It's my own hair!" Mr. Lafollie argued for a long time with the Quadra, but the only "scientific" observation he made was in regards to the alien's outfit.

Thirteen-year-old aspiring fashion designer Vivienne LaCool (that's her fashion name; she says everybody in the business has one—her real name is Lisa Jones) observed a Quadra in its vehicle when she organized a runway show at her Long Island school in 2005. "It was wearing a pathetic blouse and a hat that was truly ridiculous. Its car was awesome, though."

TECHNOLOGY

Quadra travel in sleek spaceships and listen to loud, thumping music while traveling. They do not carry any weapons or devices, only accessories, such as pocketbooks, belts, scarves, and hats.

MR. LAFOLLIE DEMANDED TO HAVE HIS PORTRAIT PUBLISHED WITH THE BYLINE "HAIR BY LAFOLLIE" IN ORDER FOR ME TO USE HIS QUOTE. HERE HE IS.

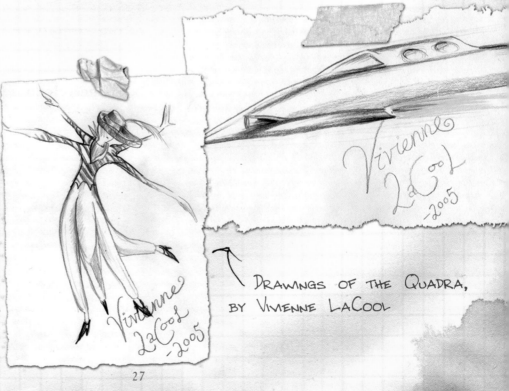

DRAWINGS OF THE QUADRA, BY VIVIENNE LACOOL

Clustor

DANGER TO HUMANS

NAME IN NATIVE LANGUAGE Unknown

ORIGIN
These aliens hail from the Great Globular Cluster in the constellation Hercules.

DIET
Clustors eat berries, fruit, and nuts . . . but most of all, they enjoy eating humans.

DISTINGUISHING FEATURES
Each individual Clustor is only 2 to 3 inches tall and dumb as a rock. Single individuals are the most commonly observed; once they start clustering together they get much smarter and know how to avoid being seen. Little Clustors eventually become huge clusters of Clustors that are able to move almost like a liquid over land, in water, and even in the air, probably with the help of some kind of psychic anti-gravity power. Single Clustors are harmless; they eat nuts, berries, and fruit that they are able to forage. But as soon as Clustors get "clustery," they start hunting for humans. If you are caught, there is little hope for you, I'm afraid. The Clustors will envelop you within their tentacles and eat every last bit of you.

THIS ANCIENT PAINTING IS BELIEVED TO HAVE BEEN AN ILLUSTRATION FOR A LITTLE-KNOWN INDIAN PROVERB THAT TRANSLATES TO: "WHEN THE DUMB GET MANY, THEY GET DANGEROUS." IT DESCRIBES CLUSTORS PERFECTLY.

These aliens are seen near lakes and rivers, especially those in proximity of berries and nuts. Most of what we know about Clustors came from the Indian crypto-zoologist Hafi Ma'ad, who spent a harrowing night in the wetlands of eastern India in 1982. He heard a series of splashes next to the cottage in which he was staying to investigate a supposed multiheaded snake. "I was dozing on a comfortable hammock, when I awoke to some splashing. I saw a small, strange being wobble out of the water and across the beach. Soon another walked out of the water and another. I counted 183 of them! They scattered around the cove and just walked in a straight line. I caught up with one being stopped by a log at the water's edge. It kept walking into it and couldn't seem to figure out how to go around or over it, nor did it notice me. But when I came upon two that seemed to have joined together, they moved a lot faster and dashed away into the forest. At this point it was late and I went back to my hammock. I slept fitfully, if at all. Then, in the early hours of the morning, I observed through the window a large cluster of them moving toward me. Before I could do anything, they crashed through the window and were on top of me, attaching little 'tentacles' to my skin. There was a terrible burning feeling on contact. I panicked and ran for my life. They followed, but I quickly jumped into my car and drove home at full speed and didn't look back."

THE BULLET-LIKE CAPSULES IN WHICH CLUSTORS TRAVEL TO EARTH

TECHNOLOGY

Clustors are launched to Earth from a giant mother ship. Individuals are loaded into a bullet-like capsule, which is then fired out of a machine gun on the ship in short bursts. Approximately two hundred Clustors are shot into a body of water at each launch. The capsules melt in water, releasing the Clustors. (They would be too dumb to get out any other way.) Once on land, Clustors seek out other Clustors with which to build a Clustor-Cluster.

MA'AD'S DRAWING OF THE FIRST TWO CLUSTORS JOINING UP

THE MACHINE-GUN THAT LAUNCHES THE CLUSTORS TO EARTH

Liverpudlin

NAME IN NATIVE LANGUAGE *Chug-a-chug-Choo-Choo*

ORIGIN

Liverpudlins are from the Railies Galaxy. The galaxy got that name because all the livable planets in the galaxy are connected with space-rails, a Liverpudlin invention that revolutionized space travel for these aliens.

DIET

The Liverpudlins eat mostly meat and potatoes.

DISTINGUISHING FEATURES

The long-nosed Liverpudlins are a humanoid species with a smaller body constitution than humans but with bigger heads and arms. They have three very thick fingers on each hand, and their hands are callused. Liverpudlins are always seen dressed in an over-the-top train engineer's outfit, perhaps inspired by their visits to Liverpool, England, in the early twentieth century.

Professor Horace Littlesens, a well-known authority on aliens, claims an avant garde team of Liverpudlins scouted Earth in the spring of 1903 and 1904 and spent a lot of time in the Liverpool rail-yards. Littlesens believes this visit had a major influence on Liverpudlin culture and led to their development of the inter-planetary rail system. The Liverpudlins probably adopted the engineer style of dress to serve as camouflage.

These aliens speak a language that sounds like nasal English but is difficult to understand.

ALIEN SIGHTINGS ON EARTH	Liverpudlins are commonly spotted near train stations, railroad tracks, or any other train or rail-related environment. They can be seen hunching under train cars, engines, or in or around switching stations, where they take notes on all technical aspects of trains.
TECHNOLOGY	Liverpudlin technology is heavily influenced by Earth's train technology, and many of the tools and vehicles that have been observed with Liverpudlins seem to be based on old designs from Earth. Their interplanetary vehicles used for local travel in the Railies Galaxy are thought to use wheels and rails, much like Earth's trains. Their intergalactic ships, which they use to travel to Earth, look like engines and do not appear to need rails or wheels.

BOTH OF THESE FIELD DRAWINGS OF LIVERPUDLIN TOOLS COME FROM DR. LITTLESENS'S DIARY, DATED 1903-04.

THEIR SPACE VEHICLES RESEMBLE TRAIN ENGINES, AS SHOWN IN THIS DRAWING BY HORACE LITTLESENS, WHO HAD ANOTHER ENCOUNTER WITH THE LIVERPUDLINS IN 1952.

THIS "COAL SHOVEL" IS PROBABLY A SAMPLE SENSOR OR MAYBE A WEAPON OF SOME KIND.

THIS "GREASE CAN" WAS USED TO SPREAD SOME KIND OF CONDIMENT ON THE LIVERPUDLIN'S LUNCH.

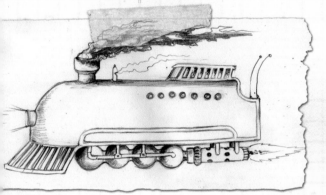

A RENDITION OF THE RAILIES GALAXY'S INTERPLANETARY RAILROAD

Zappy

NAME IN NATIVE LANGUAGE	*Zap*
ORIGIN	Zappys hail from the planet Electra.
DIET	Electric power
DISTINGUISHING FEATURES	This bird-like alien reaches about 5 to 7 feet in height and has large floppy feet similar to duck feet. Its hands look like pincers and are used to snip and strip electrical cables. The beak-like mouth is technically not a mouth but a universal connection point for electrical current.

We have never been able to communicate much with this being. The only words that it has ever spoken to a human are: I AM ZAP. At the time, this Zappy was munching on a live wire, and it added: MMMMM . . . SPARKLES. This is according to the tattoo artist Benny "The Stain" Harley, who witnessed the feeding Zappy on Route 66 in Southern California in 2001.

Even though the Zappy looks very humanoid/bird-like, alienologists believe it might actually be a mineral based life-form, perhaps nickel-cadmium based, like rechargeable batteries, since it seems able to store electric power.

These aliens like to wear outdated, slightly clowny clothes.

DANGER TO HUMANS

Zappys have been found near power stations and in places where there are downed power lines. Some alienologists believe that the Zappys actually cause storms or other natural disasters on Earth in order to feed on power lines without being noticed. For that reason, I have deemed this an extremely dangerous alien.

Ife Adebendo, a nine-year-old from Nigeria, saw a Zappy that seemed to be running out of power in her village. "The strange bird was walking down the road near my house very, very slowly, like it was sick. Then it walked into my father's garage and swallowed two car batteries, just like that, before moving quickly and disappearing."

TECHNOLOGY

The Zappys travel in extremely fast, loud spaceships that look like lightning bolts. Given that Zappys are charged with electricity themselves, it is likely that somehow they also are the energy source for their ships.

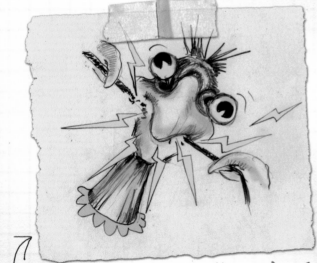

 IFE MADE THIS DRAWING ON THE CHALKBOARD SHE USES FOR HER SCHOOLWORK.

BENNY "THE STAIN" HARLEY'S FIELD SKETCH OF THE ZAPPY, WHICH HE THOUGHT MIGHT MAKE A COOL TATTOO.

THE ZAPPY SHIPS. THE BUBBLES ON THE REAR MIGHT BE COMPARTMENTS FOR THE ZAPPY CREW WHO DOUBLE AS THE SHIP'S POWER SUPPLY.

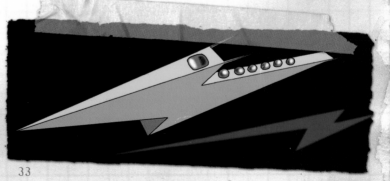

Knutt

NAME IN NATIVE LANGUAGE *Ken-utt*

ORIGIN	Knutt come from the planet Splat in the Goo Nebula.
DIET	The Knutt seem to be mostly interested in playing pranks and making mischief. There is no data on their eating habits.
DISTINGUISHING FEATURES	The Knutt is a technologically advanced alien with a wide variety of toys and gadgets. It seems as though the purpose of their visits to Earth is to play pranks on humans. These aliens are small—rarely more than 3 feet tall—and are always seen wearing helmets and goggles. Their helmets appear to have communications technology built in, and it has been hypothesized that the Knutt also have cameras that broadcast their pranks to their home planet, perhaps in the form of a humorous reality show, something like, HOW TO MAKE FUN OF HUMANS.
ALIEN SIGHTINGS ON EARTH	The Knutt are specialists at sneaking up on people and staying hidden while they engage one or several of their gadgets to humiliate humans. In one instance, retold by someone who asked to remain anonymous, a Knutt threw a stink bomb next to this individual while he was talking to a pretty girl he liked. The stink was unbearable, and none of his excuses to the girl improved the situation. The young man was utterly humiliated.

TECHNOLOGY Knutt come and go in an instant, so they must have some kind of molecular transporter technology and probably some very advanced spaceships. But all the examples of their technology that have been documented are more or less prank-related. Below are a few examples.

A GUN THAT "SHOOTS" SCARY 3-D IMAGES

AN EXTREMELY SLIPPERY LIQUID. A FEW DROPS WILL LEAD TO SLIPS AND SLIDES AND INEVITABLY, LAUGHS.

THIS SLIME-GRENADE SOUNDS LIKE LOUD FLATULENCE AND SPREADS BRIGHT-COLORED GOO.

KNUTT-TECH

WATER BALLOONS

CAMERA?

FOAM (smells like stink bomb)

MAGAZINE (changes for different ammo)

SILLY STRING-LIKE GUN

THIS IS THE TYPICAL KNUTT PRANK GUN THAT MOST KNUTT CARRY WITH THEM AT ALL TIMES.

I MADE THESE DRAWINGS AFTER INTERVIEWING AN ANONYMOUS WITNESS. HE DESCRIBED A SMALL FLYING VEHICLE FROM WHICH THE KNUTT DROPPED DIFFERENT PRANK-RELATED BOMBS (IN THIS CASE, IT APPEARED TO BE LOADED WITH WATER BALLOONS) AND A SMALL CAMERA THAT HOVERED AROUND AND SEEMED TO BE REMOTELY CONTROLLED.

IN THIS COMIC BOOK FRAME, PUBLISHED IN THE AUSTRALIAN ALIENOLOGY MAGAZINE, "WATCHING THEM WATCHING US," YOU CAN SEE THAT THE KNUTT SOMETIMES SETTLE FOR A LESS HIGH-TECH APPROACH TO PRANKING; BANANA PEELS.

HA-HAA!

Common Giant

DANGER TO HUMANS

NAME IN NATIVE LANGUAGE *Biggur Folk*
(usually said with a grunt)

ORIGIN	The planet Lore
DIET	Common Giants eat humans and other living things.
DISTINGUISHING FEATURES	The Common Giants' home planet is about 425 times larger than Earth. That number corresponds to the approximate size difference of the Giants to humans, as they are roughly 400 times larger than human men. Because of their large size, these aliens are almost never seen in full figure. The most common view is of their lower legs sticking out of clouds. They are always naked but very hairy.

Common Giants are an angry, ungenerous species. They jealously hoard valuables and smuggle them onto their ships. They have an odd sense of what is valuable. Some of the things they most eagerly collect include:
  · Birds
  · Sheep
  · Brightly colored fabric
  · Handfuls of dirt (creating hollows in Earth's landscape)
  · Gold (note the earring in the watercolor painting on right—it must weigh hundreds of pounds)
  · Diamonds
  · Towers (church steeples, castle towers, lighthouses, etc.)
Common Giants are a bit slow. A smart human can easily outwit a Giant. However, these aliens are nevertheless dangerous since they will eat us without any apprehension. To them, we are just food.

Most reports of these aliens stem from Northern Europe before the nineteenth century. Thankfully Common Giants are scarce today. The last known sighting was in Norway in 1906. The observation was made by the artist Olaf Ding, whose watercolor called "A Giant" is one of the few eyewitness accounts depicting the face of these beings.

He described his encounter in the following way: "I was hiking down the side of a steep mountain by the fjord. Just as dusk came upon me, I looked over the edge of the steep mountainside, contemplating the fragility of our existence, and lo! I was face-to-face with a giant! I hastily drew up my watercolors and sketched his portrait. He must have been full since he didn't try to eat me. He glanced at me under his heavy brows and grunted before turning away."

TECHNOLOGY

The Common Giant's ships look like medieval castles on a fantastic scale. They appear rustic, even primitive, but somehow are capable of interstellar travel. Perhaps the Giants have developed a way to use some natural occurrence, such as worm-holes (see pages 58–59) to travel in space.

The Giants have crude weaponry. They employ a club made from an enormous piece of wood.

"A GIANT." PORTRAIT BY OLAF DING

ein gotne

THE GIANT-CLUB AS OBSERVED BY OLAF DING, NORWAY 1906

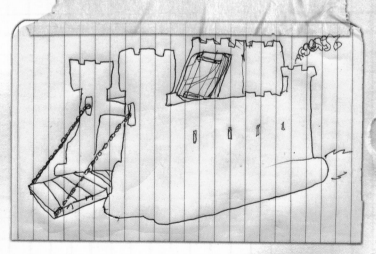

THE COMMON GIANT'S SPACESHIP. WE'RE NOT QUITE SURE HOW THIS CRUDE MACHINE IS CAPABLE OF INTERSTELLAR TRAVEL.

Glorb

NAME IN NATIVE LANGUAGE *Glorb*

ORIGIN	Glorb originate from dust clouds in the constellation Cepheus.
DIET	These aliens will eat anything round, in any material, from baseballs to meatballs.
DISTINGUISHING FEATURES	Some scientists believe that this planet-like being might actually be a baby planet. The orbiting "moons" act as the Glorb's eyes, but it is also speculated that the moons sometimes break free and create new Glorbs.

LI WANG SCULPTED THIS FASCINATING PIECE BASED ON MEMORIES OF HIS ENCOUNTER WITH THE GLORB. TODAY, LI DOES RESEARCH ON THE BIRTH OF PLANETS.

Glorb are often seen on university campuses; they are especially attracted to astronomy students. Li Wang, 20, observed one outside his dorm room at UCLA in 2007. "It was, like, just hanging in the air with these little planets with big eyes circling. I was like, 'What are you, man?' It blinked, and said 'GLORB!' Then it ate all my jawbreakers . . . didn't even chew them—just swallowed them whole!"

I observed a Glorb-raid on a Swedish smorgasbord when I was visiting family in Gislaved, Sweden, in 1998. It was Christmas and I had eaten too much and was just dozing off on the couch, when a Glorb appeared. I don't know how it got into the house. It went straight for the meatballs sitting on the table. It devoured them all and quickly disappeared. There was a bit of a kerfuffle afterward because I was the only witness and was later blamed by my brother Joakim for having eaten all the meatballs.

TECHNOLOGY

The Glorb appear to be a self-sufficient species without need for external technology. They travel in space just as they are.

A young GLORB

ACCORDING TO NASA, THIS IMAGE FROM THE HUBBLE SPACE TELESCOPE DEPICTS GALAXY NGC 7457 AND SUPERNOVA 1987A. AFTER FURTHER ANALYSIS, I BEG TO DIFFER; I'VE COME TO THE CONCLUSION THAT THIS IS PROBABLY AN IMAGE OF A GLORB BEING BORN.

MY FIELD SKETCH OF THE GLORB-RAID

Disco

NAME IN NATIVE LANGUAGE   *Boogie-dood*

ORIGIN

Discos stem from the planet Funk, which is located in a disc-shaped galaxy called Studio 55. This galaxy is characterized by a large variety of flashing, multi-colored light phenomena.

DIET

This alien absorbs beats and rhythms through its feet and doesn't eat or drink.

DISTINGUISHING FEATURES

The Disco accumulates energy from sound waves. It grows to about 4 feet tall and has an innate feel for rhythm. Whenever you see a Disco, there will be music around and the Disco will be swaying to it. It seems as if they can't help but dance. Their feet act as conductors for the beats that are the Disco's bread and butter.

The Disco's mouth plays no part in their energy intake and is used only for communication and such cheerful shouts as: "Oh, yeah!" "Boogie down, baby!" and "Get down with your funky self!" They also enjoy singing along to classic dance club anthems. It is not known if the alien actually understands what it says or if it just mimics sounds.

The Disco has a clear preference for older dance music, such as Earth's disco music from the 70s and 80s, hence its name. It is proficient in several dance moves of that era, including the hustle and the electric slide.

ALIEN SIGHTINGS ON EARTH	You are most likely to find Discos in or around night clubs, dance parties, or anywhere there's loud music.
	This alien is considered to be friendly but can be slightly annoying, according to some witnesses. Natasha Levin had an encounter with a Disco at her Bat Mitzvah in 1987 and tells how it almost ruined her party: "That horrible disco-thing wouldn't stop moonwalking. At the end of the party I wanted to dance to a slow song with Eric, and the crazy disco guy just kept sliding by, shouting 'boogaloo baby!' It totally ruined the mood."
TECHNOLOGY	Discos travel in spaceships that resemble decked-out vans with impressive sound and light systems on board. The ships have lots of antennae for sensing the presence of music on nearby planets and are comfortably equipped, with velvety lounge chairs and cushy sofas.

A TYPICAL DISCO SPACESHIP

I FOUND THIS CASSETTE TAPE AFTER INVESTIGATING A DISCO SIGHTING IN FREEPORT, ILLINOIS.

THIS UNSIGNED BUT CLEARLY DATED FIELD STUDY SHOWS A DISCO IN FULL ACTION. IT WAS SENT TO ME FROM A YOUNG ALIENOLOGIST IN COLORADO, WHO FOUND IT AMONG HIS MOM'S STUFF.

1979

Duomaws

DANGER TO HUMANS

NAME IN NATIVE LANGUAGE A long beep with an upward tone-shift: BEEEEEEEE-IIIP

ORIGIN	Duomaws are from a twin planet in a galaxy with two suns.
DIET	Any flesh, animal or human.
DISTINGUISHING FEATURES	Duomaws are a pair of individuals stuck together like conjoined twins. They are joined at the hip, literally, and share one belly. They grow to about 5 feet in height. When moving, Duomaws slither on a jelly they secrete from their elephantine feet in a way that is similar to snails, only much faster. Because of their atmospheric needs, these aliens are forced to wear their helmets while on Earth and can't eat until they are safely on board their ships. Underneath their helmets, the top of their heads have frighteningly large fanged mouths, thus their name. Duomaws can eat a small human, goat, or large dog in just a few seconds. Duomaws can grow tentacle-like arms from practically any-where on their bodies. These arms shoot out fast and are as agile as the tentacles of an octopus. The Duomaws use their arms to capture prey and transport it back to their mother ship. They can hold prey with one arm, and simply grow another arm and keep hunting if additional prey comes within reach.

The most famous encounter with Duomaws is that of Canadian arctic explorer and poet Pierre Nonbrein. Abducted by Duomaws in the fall of 1896, Nonbrein was held in captivity aboard a Duomaw ship for the entire winter. He was exceedingly well fed and had the distinct feeling that the aliens were fattening him up for a later feast. "I was so sad and lonely. I had nothing to do but eat. The most wonderful meals would come to my room, any time of day or night. I would just dream of something and next thing I knew, there it was."

Alienologists don't know how his captors were able to provide him with Earthly delicacies or read his mind.

When Mr. Nonbrein was finally released he had gained a lot of weight, and most of his friends didn't recognize him. Sadly, nobody believed his story of alien abduction until long after his death. Nonbrein never knew why the aliens chose to release him.

AN ILLUSTRATION OF THE DUOMAW'S TECHNIQUE FOR EATING HUMANS

TECHNOLOGY

Nonbrein described few notable details inside the Duomaw spaceship. He said the interior was similar to "a seagoing ship or perhaps a battleship." He saw little other technology, aside from a device "for watching electric theatre performances on a bright screen," that may refer to some kind of television. Nonbrein never saw or heard any other ships. He was convinced that the aliens used a "magical transporter-beam" to travel to and from their mother ship.

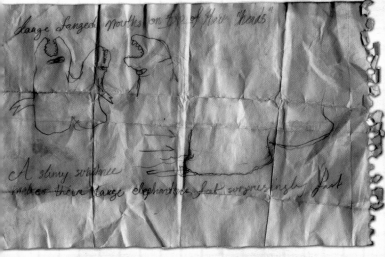

large fanged mouths on top of their "heads"

A slimy substance makes their large elephantine feet surprisingly fast

ONE OF NONBREIN'S DETAILED DRAWINGS OF HIS CAPTORS. THE NOTES SAY: "LARGE FANGED MOUTHS ON TOP OF THEIR 'HEADS,'" AND "A SLIMY SUBSTANCE MAKES THEIR LARGE ELEPHANTINE FEET SURPRISINGLY FAST."

MONSIEUR NONBREIN BEFORE AND AFTER HIS ABDUCTION

Aji

NAME IN NATIVE LANGUAGE *A'chi*

ORIGIN	A planet named Xodus is home to the Aji. It is believed that this planet is connected to Japan, probably through some kind of worm-hole in space (see pages 58–59).
DIET	Ajis eat primarily Japanese food and donuts.
DISTINGUISHING FEATURES	The Aji are a humanoid species that looks like cute young humans with oversized heads and eyes. They are slim and slight, rarely taller than 4 feet, and are always dressed in cool space uniforms. They seem to cherish the look of science fiction characters and spend a lot of time on their appearance.

The Aji also love gadgets and have an innate sense of curiosity. They are not intentionally dangerous to humans but can be by mistake, when trying to show off some new technology.

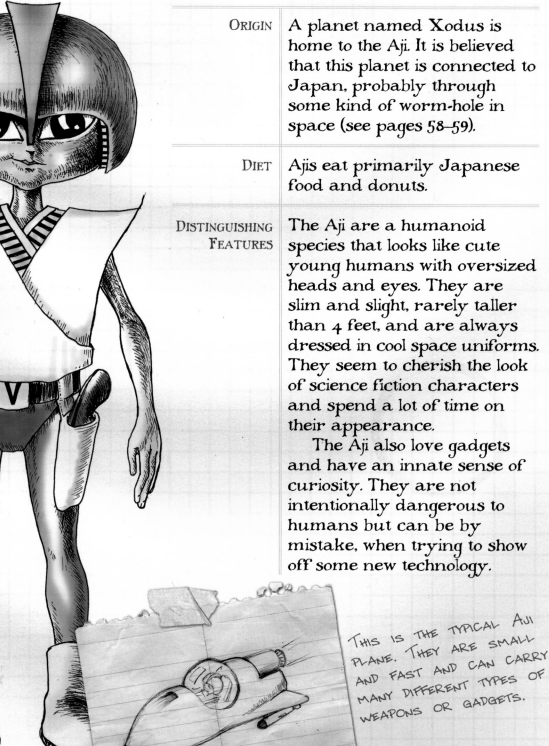

THIS IS THE TYPICAL AJI PLANE. THEY ARE SMALL AND FAST AND CAN CARRY MANY DIFFERENT TYPES OF WEAPONS OR GADGETS.

ALIEN SIGHTINGS ON EARTH

Taketo Koyabashi, eleven, from Kobe, Japan, tells of an occasion when two Ajis appeared in his bedroom and started showing him their new ray guns. The Ajis were giddy with excitement and so was Taketo. The brand-new rays could make things disappear. According to Taketo: "The aliens started shooting off the guns, and beams were flying all over my room. I thought nothing bad happened, but when I woke up the next morning, I realized that my homework had completely disappeared—not the book or the paper, but all my writing had somehow been beamed off the paper by the Aji rays."

TECHNOLOGY

The Aji are constantly developing new technology. Ray guns of different type and function are popular, and so are advanced virtual reality games and new types of air and spacecraft. Some of these devices were documented in 1963 by Japanese philosopher Ayebi Karayisi (see below).

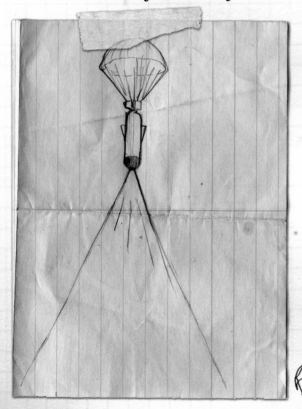

THIS FRAME FROM TAKETO'S HOMEMADE COMIC BOOK SHOWS ONE OF HIS AJI FRIENDS CHASING SOME GUINEA PIGS. THE AJI IS HOLDING ANOTHER TYPE OF RAY WEAPON THAT TAKETO SAYS CAN TRANSFORM FRUIT INTO ANIMALS. ACCORDING TO TAKETO, THE GUINEA PIGS WERE ORIGINALLY PEARS.

THIS VIRTUAL-REALITY BOMB IS DROPPED BY THE AJI FROM A HIGH ALTITUDE. IT SLOWLY DESCENDS WITH THE AID OF A PARACHUTE AND PROJECTS A VIRTUAL REALITY BEAM ONTO THE GROUND. IF YOU'RE HIT BY THE PROJECTION, YOU ARE IMMERSED IN AN ANIME WORLD, ACCORDING TO KARAYISI, WHO CLAIMS TO HAVE WITNESSED THIS FIRSTHAND AND SUBSEQUENTLY INVENTED THE ANIME STYLE OF ILLUSTRATION.

Bubblonauts

NAME IN NATIVE LANGUAGE *Blub-blub* (This is only the sound heard when Bubblonauts appear; their actual language is unknown.)

ORIGIN	These aliens come from the planet Foamo.
DIET	Bubblonauts love to eat soap, shampoo, detergents, and anything that makes bubbles.
DISTINGUISHING FEATURES	Bubblonauts are generally less than an inch tall and are most often seen wearing their bulky protective suits. Their suits are reminiscent of the spacesuits that human astronauts use. These aliens seem to be weightless. No communications with the Bubblonauts have ever occurred, apart from the "blub-blub" sound referred to above.

I MADE THIS SKETCH AFTER WITNESSING A GROUP OF BUBBLONAUTS HOVERING AROUND A CAR WASH ON 4TH AVENUE IN BROOKLYN. I FOLLOWED ONE OF THE BUBBLES INTO A PLAYGROUND, WHERE SOME CHILDREN WERE BLOWING BUBBLES. I LURED THE ALIEN OUT OF ITS BUBBLE BY BLOWING SOME MAGNIFICENT LARGE BUBBLES RIGHT IN FRONT OF IT. FOR A BRIEF MOMENT, I WAS ABLE TO OBSERVE THE BUBBLONAUT WITHOUT ITS HELMET; HE HAD TAKEN IT OFF TO BLOW HIMSELF ANOTHER BUBBLE TO SAIL AWAY IN!

ALIEN SIGHTINGS ON EARTH	Naturally, this alien is often spotted in places where humans take baths, do laundry, wash cars, or blow soap bubbles. The pre-existing bubbles give the Bubblonauts excellent cover to hide behind. The aliens can float among the regular bubbles and raid the supply of whatever bubble-making agent is available.
TECHNOLOGY	Bubblonauts fly through space on what looks like the kind of wand you would use for blowing bubbles with. It has a small rocket engine but otherwise few mechanical details, yet it is capable of interstellar travel. There are no signs of technology in their individual bubbles, although there must be some means of propulsion since they seem able to travel wherever they want to. As I observed in my encounter, described below left, individual Bubblonauts can blow their own bubble if they lose or abandon the one in which they are traveling. Their suits and helmets most likely contain communication and life-support technology.

BUBBLONAUTS TRAVEL THROUGH SPACE ON A WAND WITH ROOM FOR SEVERAL BUBBLES.

I ASSUME THAT THE JAGGED TEETH ARE SIMILAR TO THOSE YOU SEE IN REGULAR BUBBLE-BLOWING WANDS AND THAT THEY SERVE SOME FUNCTION IN BUBBLE BLOWING.

THIS PHOTOGRAPH BY MRS. SOLEDAD WAKY NEARLY CAPTURED A BUBBLONAUT IN 1978. MRS. WAKY SAW SEVERAL BUBBLONAUTS HOVERING OVER HER DAUGHTER IN THE BATHTUB, GRABBED HER CAMERA, AND SNAPPED THIS PICTURE. NOTHING OUT OF THE ORDINARY WAS CAUGHT ON THE FILM. (BUBBLONAUTS ARE NOTORIOUSLY HARD TO CATCH.) BUT IT'S A NICE PICTURE OF HER DAUGHTER ASTRID ALMOST CAPTURING AN ALIEN.

Intergalactic Worrywart

NAME IN NATIVE LANGUAGE *"Anything you want to call it"*

ORIGIN	Intergalactic Worrywarts stem from the planet Insecura, a moon-planet orbiting the much larger planet Bullia.
DIET	Intergalactic Worrywarts consume lettuce and the occasional piece of candy. However, these aliens also require an abundance of praise—a need that seems to be almost as important as food for this species.
DISTINGUISHING FEATURES	Worrywarts only grow to about 4 feet in height/length, including their tail, and can hide in some very small places. They are socially awkward. When Worrywarts get embarrassed, their pale, purplish bodies flush into an intense pink—and Worrywarts get embarrassed a lot.

48

ALIEN SIGHTINGS ON EARTH	It would seem contrary to the personality of this alien to venture out of its comfort zone, but it is actually a brave intergalactic explorer. The Worrywart has been discovered by children in backyards, play houses, and other structures that provide shelter and safety. These aliens seem to be attracted to human children. It is not uncommon to hear about encounters in which Worrywarts befriend young children by giving them small gifts and showing off their spaceships. Isaiah Carter, nine, met one but wasn't impressed. "It was such a cry baby. He gave me an apple, but I don't like apples so I said 'no thanks', and it started crying and ran back into its silly-looking space rocket. I thought aliens were supposed to be cool!"
TECHNOLOGY	Intergalactic Worrywarts fly slow and sturdy spaceships that look mundane. On the outside, they are covered with hand-painted letterings that have been translated to "WE LOVE BULLIANS" and "BULLIANS RULE" (probably signs of the Worrywarts trying to please the inhabitants of their neighboring planet).

THE INTERGALACTIC WORRYWART'S SPACESHIP

ISAIAH DREW THIS MAGNADOODLE SKETCH OF HIS ENCOUNTER WITH THE WORRYWART.

NOT EMBARRASSED   EMBARRASSED
(NOTE THE COLOR VARIATION)

Animatronix

DANGER TO HUMANS

NAME IN NATIVE LANGUAGE	Unknown
ORIGIN	This alien is an energy-based life-form that is most likely generated in empty space due to some kind of electrical event.
DIET	It is assumed that the Animatronix consumes electricity and possibly appliances.
DISTINGUISHING FEATURES	This alien takes on many forms and so cannot be identified purely by physical means. It manifests itself through the electrical machines it possesses. The old expression "ghost in the machine" probably stems from the earliest sightings of this alien.

In its most obvious form, this alien creates an "animatron" out of the various machines it possesses, making them work in strange and dangerous ways. These aliens have been known to cross wires in machines, electrify parts that are meant for humans to touch, and mess with steering wheels in cars. They have many other ways of making otherwise helpful and innocent machines into dangerous traps.

There is no known purpose to this behavior, but it is speculated that the Animatronix do some of their more mischievous activities, such as making computers malfunction, to learn how humans behave under stress, a field of study that would be of interest to alien powers who might hope to manipulate humans in the future.

ALIEN SIGHTINGS ON EARTH	The Animatronix has been seen at consumer electronics fairs and other places with a lot of electronic devices and machinery around. But Animatronix "possessions" have taken place in homes as well. I, for one, have had a fear of the vacuum in my house for years, and I think it is very likely that the infernal machine has an Animatronix inside it. It always causes trouble and has a menacing air about it. I try to stay as far away as possible from it (an act that leads to conflict in my household).
TECHNOLOGY	This species does not seem to have any specific technology but "hijacks" all matter of other technology. It is not known how Animatronix travel from one planet to another, but it is believed that they either take the form of a beam of energy and travel independently, or that they "possess" parts of space-going vehicles and travel as stowaways.

MY VACUUM, MOST LIKELY POSSESSED BY AN ANIMATRONIX

THIS FRIGHTENING CONGLOMERATE OF DEVICES WAS CREATED BY AN ANIMATRONIX THAT GOT LOOSE AT A HOME DEPOT IN PORTLAND, OREGON, IN 2008. THE COLLAGE WAS MADE BY THE LOCAL ARTIST JUDY PRINGLE, WHO WITNESSED THE EVENT. SHE TOLD ME: "IT WAS CHASING ME AROUND IN THE PARKING LOT! I'VE NEVER BEEN SO SCARED IN MY LIFE!"

Having Computer trouble?
Call the Expert Dude
I handle everything from
software-installation
to alien possession
dude@expert.com or 732 562 8020

THIS FLYER WAS SENT TO ME BY A FAN IN NEW JERSEY. IT CLEARLY REFERENCES ALIEN POSSESSION OF COMPUTERS.

Chillins

NAME IN NATIVE LANGUAGE *Brrr*

ORIGIN	Chillins come from a planet they call O-vn in a galaxy with a supernova sun (a sun that is much stronger than normal suns).
DIET	The Chillins eat any kind of vegetation, even grass, leaves, twigs, and small branches. It is assumed that their home planet is desert-like and that the Chillins come to Earth because of a shortage of vegetation there.
DISTINGUISHING FEATURES	Chillins are always bundled up in many layers of winter clothing but still appear to be freezing (another reason why experts believe they are from an abnormally hot planet). The Chillins are harmless to humans and very shy. These aliens are short in stature, rarely over 4 feet. In the few instances they have been seen without their outdoor clothing, they appear to be hairless. Perhaps that is why Chillins always wear so much fur.

ALIEN SIGHTINGS ON EARTH	The Chillins are usually seen in the tropics and deserts, or any-place on Earth where it's really, really hot. Hamid Nasif, eleven years old, of Casablanca, Morocco, observed a couple of Chillins on the beach munching on some dry twigs. Hamid claims that he communicated with the Chillins in basic French, but all they said was "froid froid," as in "cold cold." However, some researchers believe he may have just heard the crunching sound the aliens made when eating twigs.
TECHNOLOGY	Chillins travel short distances quickly thanks to their powerful jet-boots, which allow them to zoom across Earth's landscape at about the speed of a helicopter. They emit a whining sound in flight. The Chillins' ships are fairly small and give off a reddish luster to the human eye, due to the extreme heat maintained inside.

A CHILLIN SHIP. DRAWING BY IVAN TOBELIEV

THIS PORTRAIT OF A CHILLIN OUT OF HIS EXTREME WEATHER GEAR WAS DRAWN BY THE FAMOUS RUSSIAN PSYCHIC, IVAN TOBELIEV, WHO CLAIMS TO HAVE VISITED SEVERAL DIFFERENT ALIEN SPECIES ON HIS "PSYCHIC TRAVELS."

THIS PHOTO WAS SNAPPED BY 10-YEAR-OLD CHRIS OH ON VACATION IN MEXICO. CHRIS REPORTED HEARING A CRUNCHING SOUND DURING THE ENCOUNTER. HIS PARENTS SAY THESE BEINGS WERE "JUST KIDS UP TO NO GOOD." TO ME IT IS COMPELLING PHOTOGRAPHIC EVIDENCE OF CHILLINS ON EARTH.

Sliver-Slurper

NAME IN NATIVE LANGUAGE *Slurrrp*

ORIGIN	Sliver-Slurpers come from the planet Odoria.
DIET	This alien consumes waste and sewage.
DISTINGUISHING FEATURES	The Sliver-Slurper is basically an empty bag when it lands on Earth, weighing practically nothing and perhaps reaching 5 feet in height/length. As it feeds, however, it expands to colossal size. When full, the Sliver-Slurper engages some kind of antigravity device and floats up to its spaceship like a big balloon.

WILBUR GULBELL'S 8-YEAR-OLD SON SCOTT DID THIS DRAWING OF THE SLURPER FEEDING.

ALIEN SIGHTINGS ON EARTH

The Sliver-Slurper has been seen hanging around sewage treatment plants and farms with lots of animals. It would be beneficial to us to establish a firm relationship with this alien, since it eats some of the yuckiest things we have here on Earth; if they asked, we would certainly be happy to hand over our waste to them. As it is now, Sliver-Slurpers can appear quite frightening to the people who meet them.

Wilbur Gulbell walked in on a Sliver-Slurper feeding at his cattle farm's cesspool and almost had a heart attack: "I'm telling you, this thing was as big as a house, and its big, black, bulging eyes were just staring at me. It got me real scared. . . . And the stink—oh my."

TECHNOLOGY

We believe that this alien has developed full control over gravity and can float and sink according to its wishes. It does not show any visible strain under heavy loads. Sliver-Slurpers are believed to have big mother ships with large storage areas for food, similar to those on Earth's tanker ships.

I MADE THIS DRAWING BASED ON INFORMATION I RECEIVED ABOUT THE SLIVER-SLURPER'S SHIPS. YOU CAN SEE THE RADICAL SIZE DIFFERENCE BETWEEN A FULLY LOADED SLURPER AND THE DEFLATED ONES SLIDING INTO THE SHIP'S CENTRAL TOWER. PLEASE NOTE THE STINK-LINES. THESE ALIENS ARE ALWAYS ACCOMPANIED BY A TERRIBLE SMELL.

THIS IMAGE TITLED "TOWERING INFERNO" FROM NASA'S HUBBLE SPACE TELESCOPE PURPORTEDLY DEPICTS GIGANTIC CLOUDS OF GAS AND DUST. HOWEVER, I BELIEVE THESE CLOUDS MIGHT IN FACT BE SLIVER-SLURPIAN SEWER AND WASTE DEPOSITS FLOATING IN ZERO-GRAVITY SPACE. IF YOU LOOK CLOSELY AT THE OUTLINE OF THE CLOUD, YOU CAN SEE GREENISH, GASEOUS EMISSIONS. MOST LIKELY STINKY.

Andromedan Hexaped

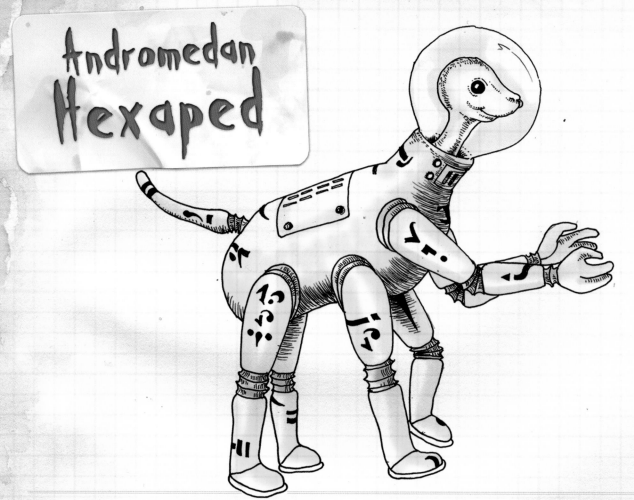

NAME IN NATIVE LANGUAGE *Ngu Ngu Bitt*

ORIGIN	The Hexapeds come from a planet they call Wroff in the Andromeda Galaxy.
DIET	These visitors will do anything for a doggy treat and like to eat fresh spring grass. They harvest the grass by cutting strips of turf and rolling it up for transport back to their home planet.
DISTINGUISHING FEATURES	Hexapeds are a species of aliens that travel in packs of eight to twelve individuals. They are always seen wearing powered space-suits, which make them extremely strong and able to fly and run very fast. They grow to about the size of a Labrador and resemble Earth's dogs in many ways (except for their extra set of legs/arms). When they are young, Hexapeds are overly friendly, like puppies, and have poor impulse control, which sometimes results in accidents. Their suits are covered by mysterious characters, part of their complex writing system, and according to preliminary translations by my multi-talented colleague Dr. Hasbien, the writings mostly concern food (see right).

ALIEN SIGHTINGS ON EARTH	Andromedan Hexapeds have been spotted in grassy areas, such as golf courses and cow pastures, in the springtime.
TECHNOLOGY	It is assumed that the Hexapeds travel to Earth on a mother ship, but the ships have never been observed.

= GIVE ME A TREAT

= I LIKE GOODIES

= YUM YUM

THIS FASCINATING IMAGE CAME FROM THE 16TH-CENTURY EXPLORER UMBERTO DE LIRIOUS' BOOK ABOUT HIS TRAVELS IN THE NEW WORLD. IT SEEMS TO DEPICT A HEXAPED WITHOUT ITS POWER SUIT. THE HUMAN SKULL AND BONES UNDER ITS FOOT ARE PROBABLY A SIGN OF THE HEXAPED'S DOG-LIKE TASTE FOR BONES.

IN EARTH'S ATMOSPHERE YOU CAN SOMETIMES SEE A PACK OF HEXAPEDS ZOOM THROUGH THE AIR IN THEIR POWER-SUITS, AS IN THIS ILLUSTRATION BY JACK FOWLER, AGE 4, OF MYRTLE BEACH, SOUTH CAROLINA. THE SUIT IS THE ONLY ITEM OF TECHNOLOGY WE HAVE SEEN FROM THIS ALIEN.

Space Worm

NAME IN NATIVE LANGUAGE   A deep, echoing *"PLONG"*

ORIGIN	Space Worms live in a group of small planets/moons in a galaxy called Orchard. They nest in the planets/moons like worms in apples.
DIET	Space Worms eat all kinds of space debris: comets, small rocks, ice, space junk, and anything that can be caught in its gigantic mouth and filtered through its thin teeth. These aliens will occasionally eat a spaceship, but only by mistake. They do not actively seek out living things for food.
DISTINGUISHING FEATURES	Space Worms are relatively rare but play an important role in the universe. Alienologists hypothesize that they are responsible for creating worm-holes in space. These worm-holes are understood to work as tunnels between very distant locations in space and time. It is believed, for instance, that the Common Giants (see page 36) and the Aji (see page 44) travel through worm-holes from their home planets to Earth. It is also thought that worm-holes might be the key to time travel.

       The Space Worms are larger than some planets, and when not in their nests, they cruise through the universe filtering space with their teeth. Their mouths closely resemble those of Earth's blue whales.

ALIEN SIGHTINGS ON EARTH	The Space Worms have never actually visited Earth but have been observed in Earth's near-space. Professor Absalom Bonkers, with the independent scientific organization International Natural Space and Alien Nurturing Environment (also known as I.N.S.A.N.E.), maintains that most comet sightings on Earth are actually the result of Space Worms swooping by.
TECHNOLOGY	Space Worms do not employ any technology but have the natural ability to manipulate the time-space continuum (i.e., creating worm-holes).

THIS ILLUSTRATION, PRODUCED BY I.N.S.A.N.E., IS A SCHEMATIC OF HOW A WORM-HOLE CONNECTING THE SPACE WORM'S HOME GALAXY TO EARTH MIGHT LOOK. THE SPACE BETWEEN EARTH AND THE ORCHARD GALAXY IS ACTUALLY MILLIONS OF LIGHT YEARS AND THE WORM-HOLE, HOWEVER SERPENTINE, CUTS THROUGH SPACE AND TIME.

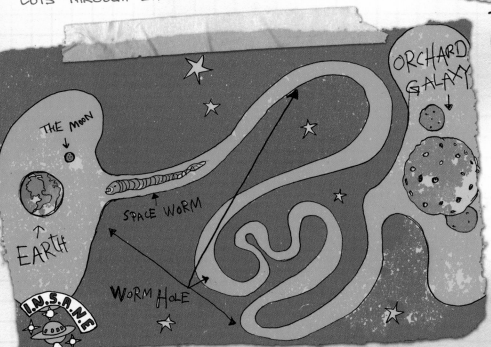

THIS INTRIGUING PHOTO WAS TAKEN BY EDUARDO DIAZ, AGE 12. HE WAS TRYING TO PHOTOGRAPH A NIGHT SCENE OVER ISABEL SEGUNDO, PUERTO RICO, AND DIDN'T SEE THE WORM IN THE CENTER OF THE PHOTO UNTIL AFTER HE TOOK THE PICTURE.

Droopian

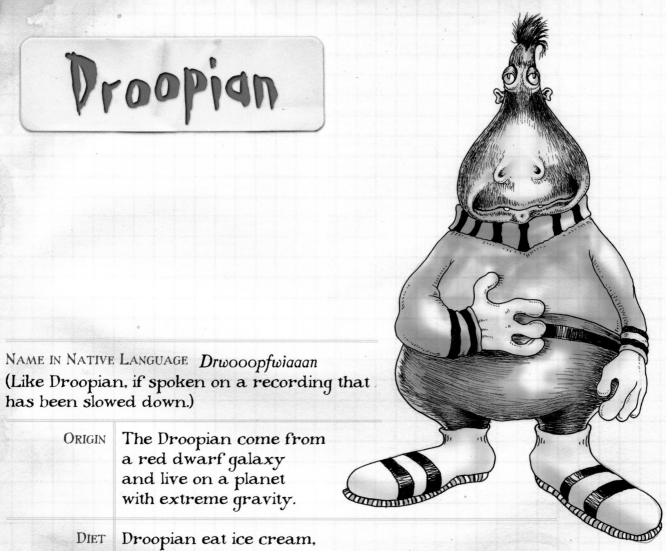

NAME IN NATIVE LANGUAGE *Drwooopfwiaaan*
(Like Droopian, if spoken on a recording that has been slowed down.)

ORIGIN	The Droopian come from a red dwarf galaxy and live on a planet with extreme gravity.
DIET	Droopian eat ice cream, cheese, and butter. They love Earth's dairy products.
DISTINGUISHING FEATURES	The Droopian are a heavyset species of small aliens. They are a slow but curious and friendly bunch. Droopian are much heavier than you would think, considering their small size. They are only about 3 feet tall, but weigh more than 2,000 lbs and have a drop-shaped body.

Droopian are talkative and speak Earth's languages, but it is difficult to communicate with them since they sound like a slowed-down recording. A simple sentence like, "Good morning, Earthling!" might take them thirty seconds to a minute to pronounce. In my opinion, the best way to communicate with the Droopian is to let them speak into a video or sound recorder and then play it back on fast forward. That way, they almost sound normal. You can do the same in reverse; record your voice and play it back in slow motion, to make it easier for them to understand you.

ALIEN SIGHTINGS ON EARTH	Droopian have been seen in the proximity of dairy farms, dairies, ice-cream parlors, and ice-cream trucks. Jesse Guffa, a dairy farmer from Wasau, Wisconsin, once sold a large quantity of milk and cream to a Droopian who gladly paid the market price in U.S. currency. Guffa had no problem talking with the Droopian, who he called "Seth."

"Well, as he was filling up his canisters with milk, Seth asked if he could use the facilities. We don't have a fancy bathroom out by the dairy, just a regular old outhouse. Seth made some pretty loud toilet noises in there, but I didn't think much of it, and we parted ways. Couple months later, I emptied the tank under the outhouse, and came upon this remarkable *thing*. It must have been Seth's doing. It weighed almost 16 pounds and was loaded with silver and copper. It was worth several times more than he paid for the milk!"

TECHNOLOGY	All Droopian equipment is built to withstand the extreme gravity of their home planet, where everything is very, very heavy. Their rocket ship has an enormous engine, which allows it to break free of their home planet's gravitational field.

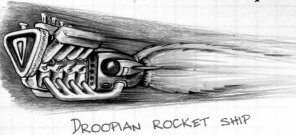

DROOPIAN ROCKET SHIP

THE "THING" THAT JESSE GUFFA FOUND IN THE TANK UNDER THE OUTHOUSE. NOTE THE EXTREME WEIGHT.

A DROOPIAN DOING WHAT IT LIKES BEST—EATING DAIRY! THIS DROOPIAN WAS OBSERVED OUTSIDE GRAETER'S, A LOCAL ICE-CREAM PARLOR IN CINCINNATI, OHIO, IN 1986 BY 16-YEAR-OLD OLIVIA WILLIAMSON. NOTE HOW "MELTY" THE ICE CREAM IS; THIS IS MOST LIKELY DUE TO THE DROOPIAN'S SLOW BEHAVIOR.

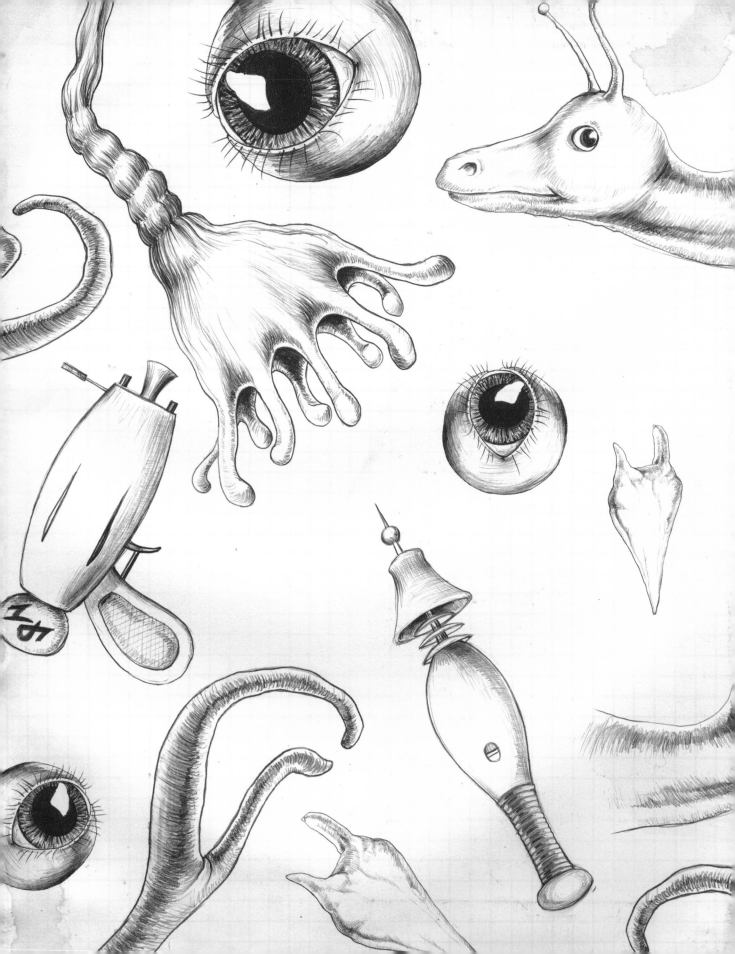